SARAH and SIMON
and NO RED PAINT

EDWARD ARDIZZONE

David R. Godine · *Publisher* · *Boston*

To my grandson Timothy

Published in 2011 by
DAVID R. GODINE · *Publisher*
Post Office Box 450
Jaffrey, New Hampshire 03452
www.godine.com

LIBRARY OF CONGRESS
CATALOGING-IN-PUBLICATION DATA

Ardizzone, Edward, 1900–1979.
Sarah and Simon and no red paint /
by Edward Ardizzone. — 1st Godine ed.
p. cm.
Summary: Sarah and Simon do all they can to help their parents, but when
their father, an artist, needs red paint to complete his masterpiece and the
art store owner refuses him credit, they do not know where to turn.
ISBN 978-1-56792-410-7
[1. Artists—Fiction. 2. Family life—Fiction.
3. Poverty—Fiction. 4. Uncles—Fiction.] I. Title.
PZ7.A682Sar 2011
[E]—dc22
2010009374

FIRST PRINTING
Printed at Toppan Leefung Printing Ltd. in China

Once upon a time there was a painter. He painted beautiful pictures, but was rather poor because few people would buy them.

When this story begins he was painting a big picture which he called his masterpiece.

This painter had a wife and three children: a daughter called
Sarah, a son called Simon, and a baby boy called Richard, but

nobody called him Richard. He was only known as "The Baby."
They all lived together in a great big room called a Studio.

Now the painter had a rich uncle who, many years ago, had wanted him to be a business man. This he had refused to be, which made the uncle so angry that he never saw the painter again, nor gave him any money.

Sometimes when the painter was specially poor, his wife would cry a little and say, "Oh dear! Oh dear! I wish you had not disagreed with Uncle Robert. We need his money so badly."

Then the painter would put his arms round his wife and answer, "Courage my dear. I will soon finish my masterpiece. Somebody will be sure to buy it for lots of money and we will be rich and famous. In the meantime, I will sell something like our silver tea spoons to tide things over."

This made his wife more cheerful. In fact, though they were poor, they were a very happy family.

Sarah and Simon slept in beds high up on a gallery at the end
of the Studio. They thought this was much more fun than sleeping
in a proper bedroom, because, from the gallery, they could watch

their parents when they gave a dinner party down below. During the day Sarah and Simon were always busy.

First they would make their beds. Then Sarah would help her

mother with the washing up, cooking and minding the baby, while
Simon washed his father's brushes, laid out his paints and made

himself useful as a Studio Boy. He hoped
that one day he would be able to paint
beautiful pictures too.

Sometimes they would both sit for their father who painted
portraits of them.

Every day Sarah and Simon would go shopping for the family.
They enjoyed visiting the butcher, the baker, the grocer, the

greengrocer, the dairy and the delicatessen, and buying such things
as meat, bread, eggs, soapflakes, cabbage, fruit, milk and sausages.

The only shop they did not like was the art shop where their father had an account. The man behind the counter was never very nice to them and sometimes he could be quite horrid.

The shop they liked best of all, though they never bought any-
thing in it, was the old second-hand bookshop into which nobody
ever seemed to go.

The owner of this shop was very kind to them. He would let them
sit in a corner so Sarah could read many lovely books out loud
to Simon.

They went here as often as they could.

In return for the owner's kindness, Sarah and Simon would help to dust the books and arrange them on the shelves. Sarah, who wrote very neatly, would sometimes help by writing down the names of the books on clean sheets of paper.

The only other person they ever saw in the shop was an old gentleman. He never spoke to the children but would sometimes give them a stern and piercing look.

One day, when Sarah and Simon were at home, they heard their mother say, "Oh dear! Oh dear! There is no money. What shall we do?"

"Courage," answered the painter, "I have nearly finished my masterpiece and then we will be rich. In the meantime I will sell my gold cigarette case to tide things over."

This, for the first time, did not seem to make their poor mother any happier.

Sarah and Simon were worried. They felt they ought to help, but did not know how. So they went to the bookshop to ask the owner's advice.

"Bring me one of your father's pictures," he said, "and I will try to sell it."

Sarah and Simon hurried home, took a picture from the studio, hurried back to the bookshop and hung it up in the best possible place.

Day after day the old gentleman would come to the bookshop. Always, he would stop and stare at the picture for so long and with such a fierce eye that the children felt sure he would buy it.

But he never did. He would walk out of the shop looking even fiercer than before, and they, of course, were very disappointed.

Now Simon had what seemed to be a good idea. "Let's be pavement artists," he said, "and make money that way."

They fetched their chalks and started work at once.

Simon made a splendid picture of a battleship and Sarah a picture of a beautiful pony. Many people stopped to look and give them money. This was success at last, when along came a policeman

who said in a gruff voice that children were not allowed to be pavement artists.

Poor Sarah and Simon were more disappointed than ever.

All this time, however, the painter had not been idle. The masterpiece was nearly finished. All it needed was a little more red paint. Better still, a dealer had seen the masterpiece and said he would buy it if it was finished by the very next day.

Alas, when the painter looked for more red paint he found

there was none left. Simon searched everywhere but it was no use.

"Children," his father said, "hurry to the art shop. Say I have sold my masterpiece and must have some red paint to finish it and that I will pay for the paint later."

But the horrid man in the shop only answered, "No money, no paint."

Sadly, the children left the shop. They did not want to go home at once and tell their father the bad news. Instead they walked to the bookshop.

Sarah took down a book and started to read to Simon. But she had no heart for reading nor had Simon any heart for listening, so they sat and talked about their problems.

What they did not know was that the old gentleman was standing behind some bookshelves quite close to them.

At last they had to go home and tell the sad news about the paint.

Their father did not even say, "Courage dear." He had no courage left himself. He had sold the teaspoons; he had sold his gold cigarette case; he had sold the clock and many other things as well.

Now there was nothing more to sell and no money to tide things over. Worse still he could not finish his masterpiece in time to sell it.

Their mother cried a lot, hugged the baby, and told her husband he must go to Uncle Robert and make it up.

Supper that night was a gloomy meal of stale bread and old cheese. Their father said nothing and their mother looked red-eyed and scolded the baby.

Sarah and Simon were glad when it was over and they could go to bed.

"This," said Sarah to Simon, as she lay in bed listening to her father stamping angrily about below, "is the end. Oh what shall we do?"

But of course it was not the end BECAUSE ——

— early the next morning they were startled to hear a great banging at the door and a great ringing of the bell. On the door-step was a rather cross-looking errand boy with an enormous parcel.

In the parcel was—

1 leg of lamb

1 loaf of bread

1 dozen fresh eggs

1 pound best butter

2 pounds sugar

½ pound coffee

¼ pound of tea

1 pot marmalade

1 large cabbage

7 pounds potatoes

1 dozen oranges

1 bottle of Worcester sauce

and A TUBE OF RED PAINT

At the bottom of the parcel was a note which read: "From a Well-wisher."

"Hurrah," said the painter, "now I can finish my masterpiece in time."

"Hurrah," said his wife, "now I can cook a splendid dinner."

"Hurrah, hurrah," said the children, because they were really rather hungry.

And, of course, they all wondered who the well-wisher could be.

The painter set to work at once on his masterpiece and, with Simon's help, it was not long before he had finished it.

It was very beautiful and they all stood round to admire it.

Sarah helped her mother to cook the dinner. She peeled the potatoes, washed the cabbage and laid the table, so it was not long before they were all sitting down to the best meal they had ever had.

They had nearly finished their splendid meal when the painter lifted his glass and said, "My dears, let us drink to the health of our mysterious well-wisher, whoever he may be!"

AT THIS MOMENT——

—— the door opened and in came the old gentleman from the bookshop.

"Uncle Robert!" said the painter. He was so surprised he could say no more.

"My boy," said the old gentleman, "I am your well-wisher. I was wrong to be angry with you all those years ago. I have watched your clever children at the bookshop and seen your lovely pictures. I know now that you were right to become a painter."

"Hurrah," shouted Sarah and Simon.

"I see," continued the old gentleman, "that you have a charming wife and a pretty baby as well. From now on I will help you all I can."

Having said this he looked at all the pictures in the studio and said, "Wonderful! Wonderful!" at each one he saw.

With the uncle's help, the painter's luck changed. That very day he sold his masterpiece to the dealer and many other pictures as well.

He became rich and famous.

He bought a cottage in the country for holidays and a large
motor car to take his family there.

But, for the rest of the time, they lived in the old studio, because they loved it. The old gentleman often came to see them and said, "Wonderful! Wonderful!" at each new picture he saw.

But perhaps their most frequent visitor was the owner of the bookshop. They were always very glad to see him.